You Can't Take a Balloon Into The Metropolitan Museum

You Can't Take a Balloon
Into The
Metropolitan Museum

story by Jacqueline Preiss Weitzman
pictures by Robin Preiss Glasser

PRETZELS 1.25
FRANKS 1.25
SODA 1.00
APPLE JUICE 1.25
HOT SAUSAGE 1.50

PUFFIN BOOKS

For our mother, Marcia Preiss, who brought us early and often
to The Metropolitan Museum, and taught us not only to look but to see

–J.P.W. and R.P.G.

PUFFIN BOOKS
Published by the Penguin Group
Penguin Putnam Books for Young Readers, 345 Hudson Street, New York, New York 10014, U.S.A.
Penguin Books Ltd, 27 Wrights Lane, London W8 5TZ, England
Penguin Books Australia Ltd, Ringwood, Victoria, Australia
Penguin Books Canada Ltd, 10 Alcorn Avenue, Toronto, Ontario, Canada M4V 3B2
Penguin Books (N.Z.) Ltd, 182-190 Wairau Road, Auckland 10, New Zealand

Penguin Books Ltd, Registered Offices: Harmondsworth, Middlesex, England

First published in the United States of America by Dial Books for Young Readers, a member of Penguin Putnam Inc., 1998
Published by Puffin Books, a division of Penguin Putnam Books for Young Readers, 2000

3 5 7 9 10 8 6 4

Copyright © Jacqueline Preiss Weitzman and Robin Preiss Glasser, 1998
All reproductions © The Metropolitan Museum of Art.
The Metropolitan Museum of Art "M" trademark and shopping bags are illustrated with the permission of The Metropolitan Museum of Art.
Matisse banner illustrated by permission of Succession H. Matisse, Paris/Artists Rights Society (ARS), New York

THE LIBRARY OF CONGRESS HAS CATALOGED THE DIAL EDITION AS FOLLOWS:
Weitzman, Jacqueline Preiss.
You can't take a balloon into The Metropolitan Museum/story by Jacqueline Preiss Weitzman;
pictures by Robin Preiss Glasser.—1st ed.
p. cm.
Summary: In this wordless story a young girl and her grandmother view works inside
The Metropolitan Museum of Art, while the balloon she has been forced to leave outside floats
around New York City causing a series of mishaps that mirror scenes in the museum's artworks.
ISBN 0-8037-2301-6.
[1. Museums—Fiction. 2. Metropolitan Museum of Art (New York, N.Y.)—Fiction. 3. Balloons—Fiction.
4. New York (N.Y.)—Fiction. 5. Stories without words.] I. Glasser, Robin Preiss, ill. II. Title.
PZ7.W4481843Yo 1998 [E]—dc21 97-31629 CIP AC

Puffin Books ISBN 0-14-056816-6

Manufactured in China

The artwork was prepared using black ink, watercolor washes, gouache, and colored pencils.
It was then scanner-separated and reproduced as red, blue, yellow, and black halftones.

Acknowledgments

The author and artist would like to thank the following people for all of their help and support in making this book possible:

At The Metropolitan Museum of Art: Kent Lydecker, Associate Director of Education; Robie Rogge, Publishing Manager for Special Publications; Beatrice G. Epstein, Associate Museum Librarian; Mary Beth Brewer, Senior Editor for Special Publications; Georgia Farber, Children's Buyer.

Bobby Pantekas, The Plaza Hotel; Steve Diaz, The Metropolitan Opera House; Michael Landers, The Stanhope Hotel; Katia Stieglitz, Artists Rights Society; Soheray Meier, Marlborough Gallery, Inc.

At Dial Books for Young Readers: Phyllis J. Fogelman, Publisher; Toby Sherry, Editor; Atha Tehon, Art Director; Julie Rauer, Designer.

Faith Hornby Hamlin, our agent; Erica Preiss Regunberg; Larry Weitzman; and our niece Yarden Fried, who had to have a balloon, and our sister Lisa Preiss Fried, who had to go to The Met.

List of works of art reproduced from the collections of The Metropolitan Museum of Art

Georges Pierre Seurat, "Invitation to the Sideshow (La Parade de Cirque)" (page 12), Bequest of Stephen C. Clark, 1960. (61.101.17)

Antonio Canova, "Perseus with the Head of Medusa" (page 14), Fletcher Fund, 1967. (67.110.1)

Jean Honore Fragonard, "Portrait of a Lady with a Dog" (page 15), Fletcher Fund, 1937. (37.118)

Hilaire Germain Edgar Degas, "Grand Arabesque, Third Time" (page 17), H. O. Havemeyer Collection, Bequest of Mrs. H. O. Havemeyer, 1929. (29.100.390)

Hilaire Germain Edgar Degas, "Grand Arabesque, First Time" (page 17), H. O. Havemeyer Collection, Bequest of Mrs. H. O. Havemeyer, 1929. (29.100.388) Photograph by Bobby Hansson.

Hilaire Germain Edgar Degas, "Spanish Dance" (page 17), H. O. Havemeyer Collection, Bequest of Mrs. H. O. Havemeyer, 1929. (29.100.395) Photograph by Bobby Hansson.

Childe Hassam, "Avenue of the Allies, Great Britain, 1918" (page 18), Bequest of Miss Adelaide Milton de Groot (1876-1967), 1967. (67.187.127)

Wedding Dress (page 19). Worn by Clara Popham Redner upon her marriage to C. Fred Richards in Philadelphia on December 1, 1880. Gift of Mrs. H. Lyman Hooker, 1936. (36.117a) Photograph by Sheldan Collins.

Mary Cassatt, "Lady at the Tea Table" (page 21), Gift of the artist, 1923. (23.101)

Greek, ca. 530 B.C., "Panathenaic Prize Amphora, Side B: Footrace" (page 23), attributed to the Euphiletos Painter. Rogers Fund, 1914. (14.130.12)

Greek, 500-490 B.C., "Panathenaic Amphora, Side 2: Chariot Race" (page 23), attributed to the Kleophrades Painter. Rogers Fund, 1907. (07.286.79)

Indian, Chola period, 10th Century, "Brahma" (page 25), Egleston Fund, 1927. (27.79) Photograph by Schecter Lee.

Egyptian, 1st Century B.C., "The Temple of Dendur" (page 26), Given to the United States by Egypt in 1965, awarded to The Metropolitan Museum of Art in 1967 and installed in The Sackler Wing in 1978. (68.154) Photograph by Al Mozell.

Jackson Pollock, "Autumn Rhythm" (page 29), © 1998 Pollock-Krasner Foundation/Artists Rights Society (ARS), New York. George A. Hearn Fund, 1957. (57.92)

John Singer Sargent, "Spanish Fountain" (page 31), Purchase, Joseph Pulitzer Bequest, 1915. (15.142.6)

Emanuel Gottlieb Leutze, "Washington Crossing the Delaware" (page 32), Gift of John S. Kennedy, 1897. (97.34)

Winslow Homer, "Snap the Whip" (page 33), Gift of Christian A. Zabriskie, 1950. (50.41)

Claude Monet, "Bridge over a Pool of Water Lilies" (page 33), H. O. Havemeyer Collection, Bequest of Mrs. H. O. Havemeyer, 1929. (29.100.113)